DRAGONCHIP

Jason O'Neil

ISBN 978-1-956001-73-0 (paperback)
ISBN 978-1-956001-74-7 (eBook)

Printed in the United States of America

CONTENTS

LIST OF FIGURES

CAST OF CHARACTERS

Ronald Miller
United States President
Age 66
Former Director, CIA
Similar to: General Norman Schwartzkopf

Barbara Miller
First Lady
Age 60 (Looks 48)
Similar to: Christy Brinkley, model

Melvin Edwards
Secretary of Defense (SecDef)
Age 62
Retired Air Force General
Similar to: General Colin Powell

Dr. Tryg Ager
Chief Technology Officer (CTO), IBM Corporation
Age 55
Internationally-known computer genius
Similar to: Robert Redford, actor

Dr. Bruce Hinkle
U.S. Ambassador to China
Age 66
Former Chairman, Cray Computer
Similar to: Eric Sevareid, Journalist

Matt Flynn
Former President, Inventor of Red Box
and Anti-gravity transportation systems
Age 81
Saved America from Socialism
Great Salesman
Similar to: Burt Lancaster, actor

Chin Chin Po
U.S. Detective based in Hong Kong
Age 58 (looks 45)
UCLA School of Criminology
Similar to: Bing Bing Li, Chinese model

Peter Wong
Detective; Life Partner with Chin Chin
Age 60
Honor graduate at MIT
Similar to: Russel Wong, Chinese actor

Sun Jei Wen
Chinese Ambassador to USA
Age 64
Embassy Bureaucrat for 30 years
Similar to: Chow Yun-Fat, Chinese actor

Mao Ling
Premier of China
Age 70
Aeronautical Engineer
Similar to: Zhou Enlai, early Premier of China

Wil Fong
Convicted spy for China
Age 35
UCLA, Computer Science
Similar to: Bruce Lee, Chinese Actor

Roy Wright
Army Colonel, Camp Casey, Korea
Age 55
Similar to: Russel Crowe, actor

Don Worsham
Commander, NORAD
Age 57
Pilot, Air Force General
Similar to: John Glenn, Astronaut

1

PENTAGON

In a secure conference room in the Pentagon, the Secretary of Defense, Mel Edwards (SecDef), Ambassador to China, Dr. Bruce Hinkle, and the Chief Technology Officer of IBM, Dr. Tryg Ager, and their staffs join a telecon with President Miller.

"Sir," started the SecDef, "I don't like the build-up of China's military. It's happening at a furious pace. They are building a new Navy complete with aircraft carriers and man-made islands in the South China Sea. Soon their numbers of ICBM's will exceed ours. They have cloned over a dozen of our aircraft. They have new submarine bases at Yulin and Xiaopingdao. So, Sir, we need a way to use our technology to leverage the huge number of Chinese students who steal our technology and return home. Did you know that the Chinese submit more patent applications annually than we do?"

"So, Mel, what do you suggest?" "The last thing I want now is a confrontation with the dragon!"

"Sir, we've been working on a scheme which could have a huge pay-off in the future, but I need your approval to proceed."

"I'm all ears, Mel. What do you have up your sleeve?" asked the President.

"Sir," replied the SecDef, "If I may, I would like to put Dr. Ager on the phone. As you know, he's the Chief Technology Officer (CTO) at IBM in Yorktown."

"Please do, Mel."

"Hello, Tryg, it's been too long," said President Miller. "I remember your tour of the Artificial Laboratory and demonstration of the Watson Computer. Sir, you and your lab are a national treasure."

The senior computer engineer and corporate executive replied, "Mr. President, thank you for those kind words. And, Sir, that's why I'm here today. At our IBM Laboratory in Tel Aviv, we've come a long way in Artificial Intelligence and have a suggestion on how to leverage this brain drain by the Chinese. Indeed, some of these bright Chinese work at IBM, soak up our technology and then disappear. As a result, we have NO Chinese-Americans in our top management. Sir, I would like to work closely with Ambassador Hinkle and Mel to use the counselor system to our advantage with your permission."

"Please proceed, Doctor," was President Miller's request.

Dr. Ager replied, "As you know, all Chinese students must have a visa to study here. We could require as part of their visa process, each person must be inoculated against flu-like viruses. Sir, our AI laboratory has miniaturized a very smart microchip so small that it can be injected via syringe. It's almost microscopic but very powerful. I just showed Mel a video which showed the shut down of a computer system once the chip in an operator is activated. In effect, it's a transponder capable of controlling systems and even provide location coordinates via the GPS satellite system."

"Tryg, that's awesome," replied an excited President. "So, if a person is at a terminal, lathe or even driving a car, the chip can be remotely activated to stop a function."

"Yes, Sir, that's right," replied the computer genius. "It means that whatever the former student is doing can be shut down. All it takes is a high-power activation command from a stealth drone or satellite. A shutdown continues until the chip is remotely disabled."

The President asked, "Do you mean to say that a bomber, Navy flotilla or even an ICBM would go dead?"

"Yes, sir," replied Tryg. "It means that no matter how big the war machine gets, a few years from now with all of the former students, particularly computer scientists, we could control most, if not all, of the devices and platforms in the country. We could hold the strategic upper-hand in negotiations. Indeed, Mr. President, a possible war could be prevented."

"Doctor, in layman's terms, how does it work and how long is the chip active?"

The IBM Executive responded, "Sir, the chip in the upper arm uses the natural electricity of the body to flow a "HALT" command down the arm and onto a keyboard. It tricks the system's software into activating the command. Once inside a system, it replicates each time the operator issues a "START" command. It's particularly effective when a group of operators is clustered around terminals in a command center and more than one chip is activated at the same time. And, sir, here's a good feature. It's inert until it gets an encrypted power-on signal. And it's harmless in the human body for a lifetime."

The President then asked the SecDef, "Mel, what happens if they find out we're doing this?"

Secretary Edwards responded, "Well, Sir, they can't deactivate the chip because it's inactive. To them it's useless. But they could stop sending students here."

"What's wrong with that?" asked the President.

Everyone in the room looked at the Secretary and said in unison: "Nothing."

"So, let me get this straight," continued the President. "At 3,000 students and 5,000 businessmen coming from China annually, by 2026, we'd have about 40,000 chip carriers in key positions throughout the country, ready to be activated in an emergency."

"That's right, Sir," replied the SecDef. "And over that period more and more capable chips will be available."

"What will the cost of this endeavor be, Mel?"

"Sir," replied Secretary Edwards, "the chip, syringe and labor won't exceed $25.00 per person or about $20M. It sure seems worth the investment to me."

"I agree," replied President Miller. "What are you calling this classified project?"

"Project Dragon."

"Very well, Mel, proceed with the project at the highest level of security and provide a status in your quarterly report," directed President Miller who thanked the audience and ended the call.

In the Pentagon conference room, there were smiles on everyone's face and warm handshakes for the Good Doctor and his staff.

2

SHANGHAI

Four months later, Ambassador Hinkle flew from Beijing to Shanghai to observe visa processing at the consulate. He got a guided tour by the Consular General to show the entire process. Consular employees interview the applicants and ask questions in English about their required essay, "Why I want to Study in America."

Proud parents of the brightest 17 and 18-year-olds from the region wait in the Cafeteria. A doctor's physical examination form is inspected for completeness with the data verified by other documents. After this two-hour process, the successful youth proceed to the Nurse's Station for a flu shot.

Dr. Hinkle asked the Consular General, "How many students are processed every month?"

"About 80 per month," was the crisp response. "And the great majority are studying computer science. Most want to go to either Stanford or Harvard. Some choose MIT in Boston."

The Ambassador mused, "And this is only one of six consulates in the country with a seventh in Hong Kong." He thought to himself: "That's a lot of spies, I mean Little Ambassadors!"

Upon his return to Beijing, Ambassador Hinkle wired a secure account of his visit to the Secretary of State who added his two-cents and forwarded it to the SecDef. He then held a dinner for a small group of Chinese agricultural businessmen who lobbied for more seeds, produce and farm equipment from America.

In his study afterwards, the Ambassador enjoyed an Arturo Fuente Opus X cigar and fine Californian Cognac, comforted by the fact that nobody in the embassy, including his wife, was aware of Project Dragon.

3

PALO ALTO

"As President of Stanford University, it gives me great pleasure to welcome you here to beautiful Palo Alto and a challenging and rewarding academic year. As new, foreign students, we hope you'll use and appreciate our new facilities and curriculum for your intellect to explore. You are a very select student body who should take advantage of all this university has to offer. Your efforts here can be a springboard to a great future, but you must make the personal commitment to excel in your studies. Please follow all directions of your advisors and counselors. They are seasoned and smarter than you!

(Polite laughter.)

This summer we cut the ribbon on a new supercomputer center. Please plan to use it creatively in your studies. You'll be rewarded with a brighter future here or in your home country."

-//-

Later that day, a dozen students from China held a meeting in a corner of the Student Union. They were so excited, almost giddy, and spoke so fast, they often had to repeat themselves! Their excitement continued later that day in a private party at Chef Wong's restaurant in nearby Menlo Park. The whole atmosphere was filled with the prospect of leveraging the American Opportunity for personal and national advantage back in the Land of the Dragon.

-//-

During the school year, the grade point average of these students demonstrated their commitment to learning as much as possible about computer-based systems. Many became expert in Artificial Intelligence and ran experiments to amaze students of other disciplines. Weekly "Data Parties" were the norm in the Union or Dormitories. Approximately one-fifth of the Chinese students held part-time jobs in computer companies throughout Silicon Valley.

On one occasion, a young man with horn-rimmed glasses and wearing faded Oakland Raiders T-shirt, dumped a backpack full of thumb drives onto a cafeteria table saying with pride: "See what I have learned in only eight short months!"

They weren't video games.

Two professors seated at a nearby table looked at each other and slowly shook their heads. Dr. Hanson was the first to speak.

"Dr. Hicks, you and I are two of only four politically conservative tenured professors on this campus. The rest of the faculty, all 1850 of them, preach and celebrate the theft of our technologies by these liberal Chinese students."

"I know. It's a tragedy being repeated at thousands of schools across this nation," replied his friend and fellow professor.

Then in a low voice, Professor Hanson said: "And this is just the tip of an iceberg."

"Victor, what do you mean?"

"It's not enough for these Chinese students to steal our technology. They have also been instructed by their Communist Party handlers to openly support the WOKE, BLM and Critical Race Theory (CRT) movements to destroy American from within by creating class warfare with open confrontations in the streets and classrooms across America."

"Do you mean the movements which seek to marginalize white patriots?"

"Yes, doctor, this whole WOKE movement is a dog whistle to call for the blacks to revolt against the perceived social injustices created by whites. And you occasionally see an Oriental victimized by a terrorist act. But it's just a smoke screen to cover the destruction of white property. The blacks are taught to shame the whites into submission so most cower in their homes while the corporations, universities and the media combine to create the new Communist state."

Pointing to the table of Chinese students, Professor Hanson continued:

"There are over 50,000 Chinese college students in America. They are ALL required to report their findings, complete with physical evidence such as a thumb drive or videotape, to the Party for application in industry and the military."

"Well, Victor, I am aware of several books which describe the reverse-engineering processes used by the Chinese to improve the technology and then use it in weapons or sell it at a lower price."

"Precisely, but there's one aspect of this situation which is also a huge problem for our democracy."

"Sir, what do you mean? Please tell me."

"Well in a few sentences I can provide some pointers for further research. First, along with the concept of WOKE, the word "equity" is used by the liberals. It does not mean "equality." On the contrary, it is a slang word used by blacks to wake-up and demonstrate in order to wring concessions from the Government for white deeds several centuries ago.

Second, CRT teaches at all school levels that the evil whites stole the black's freedom. It's even taught in kindergarten so the hatred can fester for decades.

Third, the New York Times' 1619 Project rewrites American history to put blacks at the very center of all that is Americanism. It is a racist theory to divide the nation. It even demands financial reparations from the Federal Government.

All of the above movements are "shams" to disgrace the white office-holders to hand over the keys to the kingdom to the blacks, not the Asians or Hispanics. And those Chinese at the next table are being used by the Chinese Communist Party (CCP) to whip these shams into violent frenzies, so the white patriots hide in their basements and don't challenge the New Order, meaning a Communist State."

"I really appreciate your understanding of the problem, Sir!"

"It costs over $40,000 a year to attend this university. Those Chinese students are supported by the CCP to serve as both spies and active sympathizers of these WOKE movements. The CCP also invests in the Teacher's Union, the Social-Media and the Democratic Party, all of whom educate the ultra-liberal faculties about the WOKE curriculum and its application in our society.

"So, Professor Hanson, what's the solution?"

"Professor Hicks, somehow we must stop these Chinese students from being an integral element in the Communist machine taking over our Republic. Hopefully, some technology will be invented to circumvent, indeed prevent, the use of our technologies to be used against us by the CCP. Perhaps somebody, even someone here in Silicon Valley, can invent a device, however small, which will track a student's activities and when they return to the mainland, be disabled from carrying out social or military missions against us. We can only pray something like this comes along soon, very soon. Now, let's get back to our classrooms."

4

YULIN

The southern-most province of China is the Island of Yulin with the famous resort of Sanya on the western end and the country's premier space launch center on the eastern end. Recently, a series of night-time launches of China's largest rockets caused much concern in the Pentagon.

SecDef Edwards called President Miller to report: "There's a lot going on at Sanya and Yulin. And what we don't see is really concerning. There are twenty ICBM-capable submarines in each of the twelve caverns under the island. At the same time, more and more islands are being built in the South China Sea."

"Mel, thanks," replied the President. "And we've got some of our best people on the ground there keeping tabs on the situation."

-//-

The next morning, Chin Chin Po in Hong Kong got a cryptic text: "Activate." It meant that the President wanted Chin Chin to direct one of her special detectives in Sanya to find out the truth of what was happening there using a pre-positioned network of credible sources. "Please report strength, readiness and operations by COB in 48" was the second text she received.

That afternoon, the tiny Chinese-American detective flew from Hong Kong to Sanya and checked into a 5-star resort. In a revealing red bikini at poolside, the savvy detective queried several of her sources via coded text messages from her cellphone. One-by-one encrypted notes were received on her tablet. The former fashion model turned detective quickly collected, analyzed and summarized her findings: "Massive carrier-force joint exercise planned for next month near Taiwan to demonstrate integrated communications and control. Unclear what show of force will be used."

Chin Chin forwarded the information to the SecDef. A reply text thanked her and asked her to provide an assessment of the readiness of forces on Taiwan and alerted her to come to Washington in the near future.

-//-

The next day the petite, albeit quite competent, detective returned to Hong Kong to work with her life partner, Peter Wong, to research the Chinese military situation in three locations:

- Taiwan resources and readiness given the Chinese expansion
- Bomber Bases in Manchuria
- ICBMs in tunnels under the Great Wall of China

By the end of the day, her trusted sources in Taiwan reported:

- Four new artificial islands were almost completed, each with deep water ports capable of supporting aircraft carriers. Airplanes dropped weighted flags which sunk to the bottom of the Sea thereby claiming the land for China
- Systematic, routine patrols along the primary sea trade routes
- Submarine exercises emanating from Sanya and circling Taiwan like sharks
- Autonomous drones used for surveillance of Taiwan's F-16 aircraft activities over and around the island

From her home office on Hong Kong's Victoria Island, classified messages transmitted from an antenna on her balcony were sent to various Intelligence agencies in the United States via classified satellites.

Over the next three days, Chin Chin focused on the ballistic missile threat China posed to the West. Her research also uncovered 17-airbases of which 13 support bombers from Datong, a known ICBM site, in the north to a secret base in south Yulin on Hainan Island. This facility housed a spacecraft control facility as well as a major signals intelligence facility. Many of the bases have Russian-designed Tupolev or Badger 6 bombers with a range of 3,100 nautical miles, capable of saturation bombing of Taiwan, Korea and parts of Japan.

Her sources also confirmed the ICBM inventories under the Great Wall. The estimate of 3,000 warheads was considered light due to the ability to hide railcars under the 3,000-mile length of the Great Wall. She also analyzed photographs of areas along the Wall with areas of disturbed earth which indicated missile silo tubes. The Great Wall, one of only a few man-made objects which can be seen from space, is built on deep bedrock which is considered impenetrable by most conventional nuclear-tipped ICBM's.

The Chinese detective kept asking herself, "Why does such an arsenal exist?" "Surely, no country would attack China. And the weapons are mostly offensive, not defensive. Indeed, there is no evidence of defensive missile brigades capable of downing incoming laser-guided ICBM's. These huge, new facilities are more than just employment sites for the legions of workers. There must be a grand plan for the use of the arsenal in the future."

There was no one else in Hong Kong with whom the couple could discuss their findings. During those days, she seemed so distant and couldn't even arouse her sexual libido at the opportune time. Her intellect and seasoned curiosity were consuming her.

5

HAWAII

The Hickam Air Force Base adjacent to the Inouye International Airport in Honolulu has been joined with the Pearl Harbor Naval Base to become a Joint Base. At the base is the Headquarters of the Pacific Command which supports the 15th Air Wing.

One and one-half hours north is the Wheeler Army Air Base. Only the deserted Waianae Kai Forest Reserve lies between the Army's Air Field and the Western Pacific Ocean. The site is secured by units from the Schofield Barracks and is ideal for a classified hangar at the remote western end of the air field. The hangar is operated by the Air Force and houses an undisclosed number of stealth Hypersonica aircraft for night missions over Asia, less than two hours away given the Mach 5 or 3,570 MPH speed of the aircraft.

Figure 1, Hypersonica Cover

Colonel Roy Wright commands the base, considered a stepping-stone base for promotion to General within the Army. Colonel Wright is a close personal friend of the SecDef. He is a test pilot and has flown the Hypersonica (H-1) on several missions. On a recent flight, he co-piloted the aircraft over northern China where the craft's radar picked up massive convoys of military vehicles moving east toward the border with North Korea.

His data was confirmed by a second flight a day later which uncovered the construction of an ICBM battery near the border, 100-miles west of Vladivostok, Russia and only 550-miles northwest of Tokyo across the Sea of Japan. Infrared images of the site were sent to the SecDef who immediately ordered some of his people at the consulate in Vladivostok to investigate and report back.

The report confirmed the establishment of a new missile site. What disturbed the U.S. defense officials was that the Chinese had recently fired long-range missiles capable of hitting Honolulu.

The SecDef called the President, "Sir, I smell an angry Tiger. Too many build-ups are happening at once. I'm going to call friends in to discuss tactics and strategies before I advise you."

"Good move, Mel," replied President Miller. "Just let me know when you're ready. And, please keep in mind that I'm scheduled to meet with Premier Ling in the near future. It's a lot easier to discuss things like this with real photos, the source of which I will never reveal, but, perhaps, he knows already. It's time we confront the bastard!"

The phone went silent as Secretary Edwards mulled over his strategic options.

6

ORDOS CITY

Hundreds of miles west of Beijing in the desert province of Inner Mongolia lies the deserted city of Ordos. It was built to force residents in large cities to relocate to remote areas of the country. Today, the city with its skyscrapers, opera hall and other huge venues lies empty. It's projected 1.5 million inhabitants never arrived. Indeed, a 5-star hotel room there is only $61 per night.

Over the last two weeks, there have been nights when all of the city's lights have been turned off and on several times. Either the weather has affected the local power grid, a test by the local power company has been conducted or an experiment by the military to disable the local power supply has been successful.

-//-

Informants told Chin Chin that no power system employees have been seen at distribution centers or major junction boxes within Ordos. The logical conclusion is the somebody is experimenting with a new capability such as a software application that renders an urban power grid defenseless, and thus the city goes black.

-//-

A day later, local sources reported to her that delta-winged drone aircraft were seen over the city just before the blackouts. On her balcony over looking Kowloon and the mainland of China, Chin Chin wondered out loud, "Why would the Chinese do this to their own people? There MUST be a bigger plan for the technology. But Why? And Where?"

Later that night, the petite detective gladly accepted an invitation to travel to Washington to discuss her findings.

-//-

Four days later, the pretty Chinese woman in a navy-blue silk pants suit was warmly welcomed by the SecDef in his conference room on the top floor of the Pentagon.

"Chin Chin, what an honor to again welcome you here, my dear!" said Secretary Edwards. "Your reports have been an instrumental addition to our planning. Please sit down because we have so much to discuss."

"Sir, thank you," replied the savvy American citizen stationed abroad.

"Sir, may I be quite blunt?"

"Of course," replied the Secretary. "Your seasoned word has always been of true value!"

"General. I'm really concerned that the movements in China will lead to conflict."

"So are we," replied the SecDef. "That's precisely why you're here. We need a measured response to the Chinese actions in order to prevent a nuclear confrontation."

The Secretary continued, "It doesn't get any more serious than that. My friend, the fate of the planet may lie in our decisions and our actions. Your intelligence may make the difference between the appropriate steps to avoid a disaster or blundering into an unwanted conflagration where everyone, and I mean everyone, loses."

The seasoned Chinese-American woman looked at Mel and said, "Sir, I can't sleep at night because I fear we're talking weeks, not months or years, before the situation gets very unstable."

"Chin Chin," responded the SecDef, "You're wise beyond your years!" "We conclude the same situation is upon us. I'm so glad you are here to lend your credibility to our meetings. Please plan to visit President Miller before we initiate any action, if any at all."

7

PENTAGON II

Chin Chin called Peter while the conference room was being set up for lunch with the Joint Chiefs of Staff. She was a guest and reported to her partner that "I'm in good hands, Peter. I don't think anything rash is going to happen. See you in two days, my love."

Secretary Edwards took the time to introduce the Joint Chiefs as well as other lunch guests which included two Hypersonica H-1 pilots. The party helped themselves to a seafood buffet as the SecDef started the meeting.

"Ladies and Gentlemen welcome and please may I draw your attention to the first slide at the end of the table. It's a composite of China's known military forces. It's as complete as we can make it. Now look at the next slide. You can see that many of the forces, including the missile batteries, have moved east toward the Sea of Japan."

"We are honored to have Detective Po with us today. She has served this nation quite admirably ever since her graduation from UCLA. Her network of sources throughout the Orient have been a valuable aide to our intelligence gathering. Back at Memorial Day, Chin Chin had a hunch that a major movement was about to take place. Now, here we are at Labor Day, and her hunch has come to life."

"Chin Chin, if you will, please provide some of your insight to this group which needs to know what is on your mind, my friend!"

Chin Chin got up and walked to the end of table next to the video screen. "Thank you, Secretary Edwards, for that kind introduction. I am honored to be here. As many of you know, my partner and I have had a criminology practice for two decades. But our real love is watching the Chinese military in order to provide our country with the intelligence necessary to make good decisions, most of which affect the entire planet. Peter and I attempt to put the pieces together to create a realistic picture of the puzzle."

She continued, "My friends, over the last 8-months, a clear trend has emerged. It's obvious from the current slide that a concerted military action is being staged. The equipment and personnel movements are more than exercises. There's a coordinated mission being executed. And my partner and I believe that the recent experiments with a computer worm in Ordos to control the power grid is part of any deployment or related action."

"So, detective Po, where do you see this going?" asked General Kelly, the Commandant of the Marine Corps.

"General," replied Chin Chin, "I'm particularly alerted by the increase in submarine activity and battle group maneuvers around Taiwan. Our F-16's there would provide no match for an onslaught by this Armada. The island could be encircled and a ransom demanded. And, Sir, the same is true for Hawaii."

"But we know where their forces are at all times," said an Admiral as he looked at the two pilots across the table. "There would no element of surprise."

Chin Chin responded, "Admiral, there doesn't need to be a surprise. An amassing of firepower on and below the water would warrant sizeable demands without an Allied response. It only takes one spark to ignite a blaze. Is a second Pearl Harbor out of the question? We owe China over $10 Trillion. They could call for a payment...in gold. What would be our response?"

A real buzz circled the table. The detective had ignited a number of potential scenarios discussed by the military brass.

The SecDef asked for quiet as he thanked his guest for her observations while saying, "Chin Chin, your words are very sobering, indeed, quite disturbing!"

"So, gentlemen, what should we do?" asked the SecDef. "What should we propose to the President when he meets with the Premier Ling in a few weeks? Do we demonstrate a weapon capability to perhaps dissuade China from its current actions?"

Responses circled the table:

"We could send a Carrier group to the Sea of Japan."

"We could do a Marine training exercise with the South Koreans."

"We could do F-16 drills over Taiwan."

"We could demo an anti-missile laser over Hawaii."

"We could refuel a submarine at Vladivostok."

Other ideas were floated before the SecDef said: "Or we could do nothing and provide a picture to the President to show the Premier. It would shout: "Don't make a foolish move!" But, what ever we do, we don't want to unduly alarm our citizens at this early stage."

The meeting ended with no specific military direction given by the SecDef. But he directed his planners to continue to develop scenarios and potential responses.

Later that afternoon, Secretary Edwards called Dr. Ager at IBM.

"Tryg, I'm so glad we have Project Dragon in operation. My hunch is that we will need it sooner rather than later. Please keep me posted on any updates."

The telecon ended with, "Of course, Sir, you'll be the first and only one to know."

8

NORAD

"Welcome, Cadets, to the North American Defense Command or NORAD here in our very secure underground command center. I was honored to be your Graduation Speaker, and now, proud to be your tour guide today. Plenty of our staff can provide a great tour. I wanted to do it today in order to stress the uncertainty in the world as you assume your duties worldwide in the Air Force."

About 2-dozen recent graduates stood in the gallery overlooking the command center with it huge wall-to-wall video displays and 3-dozen people seated in front of multiple displays on their desks.

General Don Worsham continued, "As you learned in your classes, the Cheyenne Mountain Complex here in Colorado Springs, Colorado has multiple responsibilities in this mountain hideaway. We must be aware of whatever is in our air space that potentially could pose a threat to our citizens. This responsibility involves the coordination of fighter jets, bombers, alert Aircraft like AWACS, and provide spacecraft data downlinks. Some of the officers and technicians you see are from Canada as our trusted partner. Indeed, just yesterday, we ran joint exercises out of Elmendorf Air Force Base in Alaska with aircraft from Canada. We also help plan and assist where necessary with missions of the Strategic Air Command and the Space Command. As we walk through the facility, please hold your questions until the end. I ask this because so often most questions are answered on the tour, a tour I took only 36-years ago!"

There was a polite giggle in the gallery.

The General continued, "So, my fellow blue-suiters, please follow me over to station 1, the Communications Center."

As the group was walking over to the Center, a Colonel pulled the General aside to alert him to an "incident" which should demand his attention.

"Ladies and Gentlemen, I'm sorry, but you'll have to excuse me, duty calls. Colonel Angie Roberts, here, will be your guide for a while."

The General Officer quickly disappeared down a corridor as the Colonel resumed the tour. Escorted by four staff members, General Worsham entered the Combat Information Center (CIC) to be briefed on the particular incident. Only a minute later the group was standing in front of a monitor watching a video of a missile launch.

A technician spoke: "General, Sir, this is video from a Hypersonica only 20 minutes ago. It shows a medium-size ICBM launched from north central China over North Korea and ultimately splashing into the Western Pacific, 900 miles west of Hawaii. Our initial assessment, Sir, is that it was a test vehicle with a problem."

General Worsham asked, "Captain, how certain are you that it was only a test?"

The Captain replied, "Sir, the heat signature of this vehicle is from a previous generation of Chinese missiles. It certainly didn't have the range to hit Hawaii. One guess, Sir, and it's only a guess, is that they use these old missiles to re-activate old missile sites or commission new ones. The Chinese can claim that there are no warheads."

The General responded, "Captain, I've seen this before, and I think you're right."

General Worsham than turned to an aide and instructed her to "notify all interested parties." She knew it meant the Pentagon, forward bases in Asia, the Strategic Air Command and the Space Command.

Then the General turned around to ask another question of the Captain, "Captain Boyle, do I assume correctly that given the speed of impact, there would be no debris of interest floating on the surface?"

"Yes, Sir, our Navy would find nothing," was the right answer.

The General asked his aide to keep him informed of any related or other incidents as he quick-stepped down the hall to join the tour just in time for questions.

9

MASSACHUSETTS

"Lu, hurry up, we'll miss our bus and be late for the Happy Hour."

"Wen, calm down, I need to pack my laptop and a couple thumb drives in my backpack. I'll only be a minute. Why don't you feed the fish while you're waiting?"

Minutes later the two Chinese women were sitting next to each other on the bus for the one-mile ride to the local pizza parlor, called Area Four, where the Chinese Student League (CSL) meets every other Friday night. The restaurant is only 4-blocks from the famed Massachusetts Institute of Technology (MIT) Media Laboratory, a Mecca for computer scientists in America. On alternate Fridays, the CSL meets at the Sumiao Hunan Restaurant on Third Street for cocktails and dinner.

The topic for tonight's meeting is "CYBERSECURITY-THE WORM'S DILEMNA."

About 30 MIT and 10 "Aliens" from Harvard routinely meet to discuss computer technologies. Students from Taiwan and Hong Kong are not allowed in this group of "Mainlanders." They meet every week to cross-fertilize each other on topics such as:

- How to break into "secure" on-line systems
- The design and activation of Worms and Timebombs
- Creation and avoidance of Trapdoors
- Creation of "Brushfire' code to debilitate a computer system
- Creation of "Smoke Screens" to avoid detection of the source of worms
- Creation of "unbreakable" encryption schemes

Once in a while, the League invites an MIT faculty member to help legitimize their activities as an "extension of their laboratory work." They routinely quiz the instructor on the best places to work where they can get the broadest exposure to cyber science. Most wanted to go to universities with liberal faculties which would not interfere with their research or part-time work. Some wanted to go to industry where supercomputers are routinely utilized. IBM was, and continues to be, a leading candidate. Many wanted to be DoD-contractors near Washington, D.C. with the many cyber labs surrounding the Capital.

Nobody talked about marriage or becoming an American citizen. All were required to return to the mainland within two years or family members would suffer the consequences.

Every Fall, the new Chinese students were inducted into the CSL, quizzed about their expertise and directed into particular curricula. Over the decade, more 2,600 cyber experts left MIT, with or without a degree, gained experience in American industry and returned to China as "loyal" Mainlanders.

Just as in Palo Alto, these students are also enlisted by the CCP and used by the liberal professors to support the WOKE movement of class warfare. The students take part in marches, rallies, seminars and held frequent meetings in the student union to assess their progress. Selected African-Americans are brought to their "Yellow Circle" to learn the latest tactics to "conquer the White Supremacists." Several of the students create applications which clandestinely cut-off on-line discussions between conservative parties. All too often an "electrical storm somewhere along the network" is used as an excuse for the lost connection. Many of these weapons are used in other countries by the CCP because they helped build the national communications infrastructure under a low cost, Debt-Trap program.

Chin Chin Po and Peter Wong and their associates followed the careers of many of these experts as they rose in the ranks of the Communist government, with many required to serve in the military. To the couple, the prospect of Cyber Warfare with America was inevitable. Chin Chin was determined to predict the time, place and nature of the attack. She thought to herself: "Fortunately, Project Dragon is very much alive with occasional, but undetected, microburst activations of selected chips to test communications links."

10

ANNAPOLIS JUNCTION

Only two weeks after the Chinese missile launch, a military tribunal at Fort Meade in Annapolis Junction, Maryland, pronounced Mr. Wil Fong, a contractor with a major defense firm, guilty of espionage by the Defense Information Systems Agency (DISA), collocated at the Army base. Over a three-month period, computer systems engineer Fong systematically copied Top Secret data files while working the night shift at a cybersecurity laboratory on the base.

The prosecution had an "ironclad" case against the defendant, complete with videotapes, voice prints, finger prints, retinal scans and a cache of thumb drives.

The defendant was captive in the brig while the 6-month trail including an Article 32 Probable Cause Hearing per the Uniform Code of Military Justice through pre-trial hearings, jury selection, arguments, deliberation and sentencing.

The defense counsel, or Judge Advocate, had little or no defense. It only took the Jury one hour for the Foreman to announce "Guilty" on all counts. The serious charge of "spying" could result in the death penalty.

A call was placed to the SecDef, "Sir, we have a guilty sentence in the Fong case. What shall we do?"

The SecDef replied, "I don't want a confrontation with the Chinese. Confiscate all of the defendant's property for analysis by the Intelligence Community, revoke his passport and visa and put him on the first plane to China."

"Yes, Sir!"

The SecDef then instructed his staff to contact the Chinese Ambassador with a very stern warning to his counterpart in Beijing.

-//-

That night, before a roaring fireplace in his den at his home in Alexandria, Virginia, the SecDef sipped a brandy and thought to himself, "This Fong guy is probably the tip of an iceberg. I wonder how he got a Top-Secret clearance on a student visa. I wonder just how many more Chinese Nationals are in this country, all with the evil intent of serving the Dragon to slay America. I think I'll start an investigation. The findings would at least make for a good spy-thriller book in the future."

11

WHITE HOUSE

The SecDef and his key intelligence staff members met with President Miller in the Situation Room in the basement of the East Wing of the White House.

"Mel," began the President, "your call was disturbing. Show me some of the evidence. I need to be "armed and dangerous" for my meeting with Premier Ling next week in Vancouver.

"Yes, Sir," replied the SecDef. "Colonel Wright will brief our slide deck. Roy, you've got the microphone."

The senior Army Colonel, Commander of Camp Casey in Korea, showed the visual evidence of the Chinese military build-up, movements and maneuvers on the East Coast of the vast country. Night time photos showed railcars exiting the Great Wall tunnel. Two newly-commissioned Aircraft Carriers were conducting exercises just outside the territorial waters of South Korea and Japan. Drones were videoed flying over Taiwan.

"And, Sir," said the colonel, "please look at this before and after of the city of Ordos. It appears to be an experiment of a computer virus to disable the power grid, even a redundant one, for the city,"

"So, Sir, why would they go through all of these actions, if they didn't intend to conduct a military mission?" asked the SecDef of the President.

"Mel, that's a very good question. And I'm thankful for the H-1's, developed by Matt Flynn, are able to gather this much intelligence without detection. Thank God, the Chinese have never been able to reverse-engineer or develop a Red Box anti-gravity device. The world would be a quite different place if they had this Earth-shaking device that make so many new aircraft possible," said President Miller.

"Mel, please clear the room. I have a question for you alone."

Only a minute later, the two friends and confidants were alone as the President pushed the off-button on the recorder.

"Mel, before I meet Premier Ling, I need to know that Project Dragon is fully operational. I can't afford surprises," said the President.

The SecDef quickly replied, "Sir, it is fully operational. At last count, we have over 4,000 implants in high positions, most in the military. Even that spy, Fong, has returned to his duty station aboard a submarine."

"Excellent, Mel, that's exactly what I needed to know."

President Miller continued, "We're talking about a potential nuclear showdown. I don't want another Cuba. I want to put the fear of Buddha or Confucius, I don't know which one, in the Premier's mind, such that, even if he has some demonstration of strength, he goes home with an "Oh, Shit" reality check. Too much is at stake. Do you know what I mean, Mel?"

"Sir, you have my word," replied former General. "We're ready. Tryg is smiling at the opportunity to prove it!"

"Thanks, Mel," "This briefing is over. Please thank your staff and join me in the library for an adult beverage."

12

VANCOUVER

The Canadian Prime Minister welcomed Chinese Premier Ling and President Miller at the Pan Pacific Vancouver Hotel on Canada Place Way only one block from the Convention Center on Pier 6 on Vancouver Harbor. A regal state dinner was hosted by the Canadian Royal Mounted Police in their brilliant red uniforms. It was a gala affair with multiple champagne toasts for tri-party friendship and mutual trade alliances. Canada wanted to sell wheat. The Chinese wanted hogs, and the Americans wanted to sell Kentucky Fried Chicken.

The next morning, the President and the Premier toured the Convention Center filled with Chinese agricultural products-everything from animals to columbines to seeds, from a country eager to export food while feeding billions of citizens.

In the afternoon, the wives toured Stanley Park to celebrate the international display of Totem Poles and a new Bonsai Tree exhibit. Both ladies had intense interest in the science and beauty of the trees and seemed to enjoy each other's company during the event. Also, in the afternoon, the Prime Minister excused himself to commission a new Ferry Service to North Vancouver.

-//-

As requested by the President, he met the Premier and his interpreter as the foursome strolled through the Nitobe Memorial Japanese Garden without the press. The President, who trusted his interpreter from prior meetings, was polite but very direct.

The President opened the dialog, "Premier Ling, our two countries need each other for our economies, indeed, our lifestyles to continue. It would be a disaster of monumental proportions if an armed conflict between us were to take place."

The Premier, with a coy smile on his face, replied, "Sir, I'm not sure I know what you mean."

The President replied, "Sir, do you remember the famous Yalta meeting after World War II?

"Yes, but….."

"At that meeting," continued President Miller, "both Churchill and Roosevelt knew that the Russian Stalin was a liar who wanted to conquer the world for Communism."

"OK, Mr. President, but we're 80-years later. What's your point?" asked the Chinese leader.

President Miller was quick to reply, "I see history repeating itself."

Premier Ling asked, "Sir, with all due respect, what do you mean?"

President Miller stopped walking and turned to face the Premier as he said, "What I mean is quite simple, Sir. And for your ears only, we have observed your military build-up with grave concern. Why else would you do it except to try to crush America on behalf of Communism?"

Only the birds could be heard chirping in the background.

"Why would I do that, Sir" replied the Premier. "My armies are peaceful."

President Miller was quite direct, "You could conquer to reclaim the Trillions of dollars we owe you on behalf of your people and keep your personal grandiose lifestyle. May I please continue?"

"Please do so Mr. President, but I don't see where our conversation is productive."

The President reflected a moment before saying, "History has shown that ALL Socialist Communist States, and, quite sadly, ALL Democratic Republics fail after about 200-250-years because of undelivered promises to the masses. Today, we're both at that point. American needs trade to keep the economy afloat. China has very few internally-developed products to trade. Therefore, you need war on many fronts, including the cyber-front, to conquer the riches of others!"

"Well guess what?"

"What?"

"We're not going to allow it to happen. You can threaten military action for ransom. It won't be paid. You can demonstrate some kill scenario. It will be matched in kind and then some. Your embarrassment may lead to a unified response including nuclear weapons. The debris in the atmosphere kills the planet. Fortunately, Sir, it will never get to that Doomsday!"

The fluster Premier responded, "I have much more power than you can imagine!"

The President resolutely responded, "No, Sir, you don't. I know where ALL of your assets are and their capabilities."

"Oh, how is that possible? You're lying like Stalin!" replied the Premier.

"Oh, it's not only possible," replied President Miller, "but you can believe me. I won't have to fire a single weapon to stop any attack. Period. This is NO bluff. Only fools bluff when it comes to nuclear war."

The President came to a conclusion, "You try one, only one act, and I'll shut it down before even the lid of a missile silo is opened. Is that clear?"

"It's clear, but unproven, Mr. President. And you're no Roosevelt!"

The President smiled and said, "Thank you, Sir, I'll take that as a complement."

He continued, "Fortunately, I have my health, wit, and weapons to back up my claims! Nuclear war will not happen on my watch. And, for God's sake, I hope you're no Stalin! Go home. Turn the war machine around and make tractors. Our John Deere needs some competition!"

The translators looked at each other and shook their heads as if to say, "I don't believe what I just heard, but I'll remember it for the rest of my life."

-//-

The banquet that evening was cancelled by the Premier.

The President and Mrs. Miller had dinner alone in their suite.

Barbara commented, "Honey, you're spooky quiet tonight. I hope everything is alright."

"My dear," replied a loving husband, "I'm just tired from playing a chess game with so much on the line. At some future date, I'll explain. It has to do with very tiny smart computer chips, and I must leave it at that."

The First Lady responded, "I trust your decisions, Ron. After all, you married me!"

They clinked wine glasses as the Earth continued to turn on its axis.

13

HAWAII II

Two months to the day after the President's meeting with the Premier in Vancouver, at sunrise on a summer Sunday, a radar operator at a remote post on the island of Kauai in the Hawaiian Islands, noticed unusual submarine activity in the Pacific Ocean 200 miles west of Honolulu. While looking at his radar scope, he called his duty officer, "Sir, I think you should look at this."

"Sailor, what do you see?"

"A large pod of metal whales, Sir," was the answer.

"The officer responded, "I'm driving up to the site now and will be there in 3-minutes or less."

-//-

"Sailor Brown, you're right" said the Ensign as he peered at the scope while dialing his cellphone.

"Commander, this is Ensign Burnham, we have an alert, please search the area with the following coordinates…."

"Thank you." The phone went dead.

-//-

Within a minute, the whole power grid serving Honolulu went dead. Back-up generators turned on all over the city. Classified communications links, however, were not disturbed and communications with the Mainland via satellite continued.

On the television, an Asian woman spoke fluent English, "Your country has 36-hours to transfer $1 Trillion to the address on your screen, or additional actions will be taken."

The President and Mrs. Miller were having lunch in the White House when the urgent call came in.

"Mel, what's up?"

The SecDef replied, "Sir, the Chinese have disabled the power grid serving Honolulu and are demanding a $1 Trillion ransom or else."

The President had a flashback to World War II when an American general answered a surrender demand from the Nazis by saying, "Nuts!"

"Sir, we have 36-hours to respond," continued General Edwards.

"Mel, bring your Tiger Team here for a meeting in the Situation Room at 1500."

"Yes, Sir." The phones went dead.

-//-

At 3:00 PM, the Situation Room was crowded with top military and civilian leaders. Members of the Intelligence Community lined the room. The President walked in and sat down at the head of a long conference table and asked, "Mel, what's the latest report, and what are our options in this "or else" scenario?"

The SecDef replied, "Sir, it is our opinion that the C-7 Grid was attacked by an aggressive virus, probably activated when a submarine surfaced. Our team, including Dr. Ager, located the virus and neutralized it a half-hour ago."

"Excellent!" replied the President. "What's happening under the water?"

Admiral Cochran spoke, "Sir, the pod has dispersed and is heading west, all except one submarine that has been circling in the same region at a depth of 1,300 feet."

The President then said, "I have instructed Ambassador Hinkle to deliver a one-word message, "Nuts!"

A polite "at-a-boy" went around the room.

The President continued, "In my meeting with Premier Ling, I made it crystal clear that we would respond immediately to any act of aggression. I believe this was a shot over the bow to signal further acts which would comprise the "or else."

"Unless there is universal, reasoned disagreement in this room, I believe we must respond in kind."

The President paused and looked around the room before asking, "Is satellite KH-26 on station?"

A slight man with round horn-rimmed glasses in the background replied, "Yes, Sir, it is."

The President than directed, "Activate a Dragon aboard the submarine, and we'll show them we mean business and go to DEFCON II."

Most in the room did not know the meaning of "Dragon" but knew that if a major satellite was involved, it would most likely be very effective.

Within an hour, a Sonic Stealth Drone (SSD) was hovering over the submarine ready to drop a tracking pillbox for attachment to the submarine to activate a Dragon(s) inside upon command from the satellite. The Commander at Schofield Barracks issued the command approved by CINCPAC. Within six minutes, the sound of the submarine's propeller screws ceased. An engineer in the SSD control center reported, "She's dead." Colonel Wright knew that the helpless craft was sinking to a watery grave.

The SSD returned, landed safely, and quickly crossed the tarmac into its camouflaged hangar.

14

BLAIR HOUSE

One week later, President Miller called Hong Kong to request that the "Sleuth Couple" come to the White House for a private meeting about the developing crisis with China.

Within 12-hours, a Hypersonica landed at Dulles Airport. A black Suburban picked up the couple and took them to the Blair House. This 280-year-old townhouse a block north of the White House has seen many prestigious guests. Chin Chin told her partner about the many famous people who stayed there.

Peter asked, "Who is Marilyn Monroe?" Chin Chin simply put her finger to his lips and said, "Sheee."

The couple enjoyed the evening in front of a small fireplace, sipping brandy and massaging each other. As their loins grew more excited, they jumped into the very bed used by Winston Churchill to consummate their love.

In the future, they always remembered these moments of sheer joy.

-//-

At 8:30 the next morning, the couple was enjoying breakfast with President Miller.

"Chin Chin and Peter, I need to know what is going on in Premier Ling's mind, said the President with an urgency in his voice. Has the event fed his ego, or are more moderate actions to prevail?"

Peter was the first to respond, "Sir, Chin Chin and I watched this build-up over the past 4-years. We have reported on it every quarter on schedule. Chin Chin has made several presentations at the Pentagon. Today, I can say with confidence that there is an attitude to start a war. "Our brave soldiers will be able to win it!"

Peter continued, "But, Sir, the recent event has shown them that they really do not understand the nature of combat in this era. There are no battle lines of troops as in Greece, Rome, Waterloo, Gettysburg, World War I and II, and Korea. Today's war is fought with surrogates like robots, drones, UAV's, Ghost Ships and a host of cyber-created decoys, most much smarter than the Generals!"

The President quickly responded, "Peter, you're right. But we have a potential nuclear exchange in front of us. What does the modern Chinese logic say about the prospect?" asked President Miller.

"Sir, let's look at history over the last 500-years. The Great Khans would advance to destroy an enemy. The Ming Dynasty, used many weapons, especially torture, to subdue an enemy. In the last century, Mao Tze Tung used propaganda to rally his forces. In the last 50-years, the Chinese have supported the expansion of systemic control just like in Vietnam. Today, the Premier feels he can win on all levels but is really confused about which direction to take in the new cyber world."

That's all good, Peter, but what about their confused mindset in the Nuclear Era?" asked the President.

"Sir," said Chin Chin, "what Peter is saying is that the Chinese military have great difficulty grasping a cyber enemy. The youth understand it, but the senior military leaders still want to apply legions of troops."

"So?" asked the President.

"So, Sir," continued Chin Chin, "our advice to you is to keep the pressure on them. The senior military leaders do not know how to respond in a nuclear environment where one false move destroys all of the troops, assets underground and afloat, much less the planet."

"So?" asked the President a second time.

"So, Sir," answered Peter, "America needs to demonstrate that we are much smarter than China and are able to neutralize any move they make such that it sinks in: "We, China, will end life on Earth!"

Peter continued, "Let me say, Sir, that when they lost that submarine, their very newest and most capable, it sent shock waves through the entire military. No shots were fired, but they lost a submarine and 140 people on board from an invisible enemy they don't understand. They are still asking, "How is this possible?"

The President then asked, "Can you give me some options in priority sequence, of what the Chinese would do next?"

Chin Chin spoke, "Mr. President, based upon our network of sources from all over China, the people do not want to go to war. Unlike the current regime, feeding a family of four is a daily struggle. The grassroots people really resent the military as "leaches taking advantage of bureaucrats willing to spend other people's money and lives."

"So?" again the President pressed for savvy advice.

"So," replied the smart detective, "If Thomas Jefferson were alive today, he would say: "I told you so!"

Just then, an aide rushed into the breakfast cupola and whispered in the President ear. The President quickly rose out of his seat and said, "Sorry, but this breakfast is over. I must attend to a very urgent matter. Please remain in Washington, only a cellphone away."

Chin Chin and Peter's eyes met as the President rushed from the room. Peter asked: "What could be more important than Nuclear War?"

Chin Chin said, "Nothing."

15

THE CALL

With the President seated at the end of the table and key military and civilian leaders on both sides and the walls lined with aides, the President nodded to put the Chinese Premier on the speaker in the Situation Room.

"Mr. President it is with utmost urgency that I call you and request your country's assistance."

"Premier Ling" replied President Miller, "What has happened, and how can we help?"

"We've had an accident at one of our missile sites."

The President asked, "What is the situation, and where did it happen?"

The Premier replied, "A missile was armed by mistake at the Anshon site, 75 miles west of North Korea."

There were many nodding heads around the Situation Room.

The President asked, "Accident or was it being prepared for launch?"

Many in the room took a deep breath; some hearts skipped a beat.

"We call it an accident, Sir!

The President then said, "Sir, this is very grave. That site is at the end of the Great Wall. As I understand it, you've got some 3,000 nuclear warheads under the Wall.

Is that right, Sir?"

The Premier was coy with his answer, "We have many."

"Well, Sir, the President continued, "If we have a chain-reaction, and many missiles explode, the debris cloud could block out the sun!"

"You are correct, Sir. "That is my understanding as well," replied a rattled leader.

"Have you notified the United Nations, Sir," asked the President.

"Yes."

"What do you want me to do?" asked the President. "After all, you recently had a hostile military act against our State of Hawaii."

"Mr. President, does your country have the ability to disarm a nuclear missile remotely?" asked a very nervous Premier.

"Premier Ling are you testing us, or is this a real potential disaster?" asked the President.

The silence in on the line and in the room would never be forgotten by the participants.

The Premier regained a strong voice and replied, "Mr. President, I remember your warnings in Vancouver. I wouldn't call if it weren't a true emergency. Somehow we must shut down or override the control system which our engineers have been unable to do."

"How much time do we have, Sir," asked the President in a potentially deadly silence.

"The current estimate is 4-hours before the failsafe mechanisms will be exhausted."

The President was very quick to respond, "Sir, no promises, but we'll take immediate action. And, Premier Ling, should we be successful, I will insist on a missile draw-down treaty between us. Do I make myself clear?"

Premier Ling responded, "Yes, I understand and will comply."

"Thank you, Sir," replied President Miller. "We will keep this line open for further updates and actions. May the Chinese people be forever grateful for your courage at this time."

-//-

The President nodded to General Edwards to make the call to Camp Casey in Korea to dispatch an SSD immediately with the appropriate Dragon activation codes. Two satellites were on station as backup, but their downlink signal would not be as strong as the signal from a drone hovering only 100's of feet above the silo.

Colonel Wright estimated the ETA at 38 minutes. Nobody left the room; many perspired in place.

Less than twenty-minutes after the call, a video feed came in from the drone. A secure voice channel from Camp Casey could be heard in the background.

The audience in the Situation Room, most of whom which had no prior knowledge of Project Dragon, quickly figured out what was, hopefully, happening.

The President and senior staff were glued to the speakerphone in the middle of the table.

Colonel Wright's voice was clear, "Vehicle in place; Request activation."

The President pointed his finger at SecDef Edwards, who said, "On my count, activate: 3,2,1, activate."

During the anxious moments which followed in the Situation Room, the SSD broadcast a coded signal and was immediately commanded to return to the base. It turned north over Manchuria and crossed over the deserted Nanfen District on a southern course past the city of Dandong.

As the SSD was half-way back to Camp Casey, the Premier's voice could be again heard on the speaker.

On the other end of the line, a translator had difficulty, but the words came through: "We have confirmation of the complete shutdown of the missile. Mr. President, we do not understand your technology that just enabled this feat. But the leadership at the site, here in Beijing and the Chinese people are truly grateful. I will notify the Security Council of the United Nations. My Ambassador will be in contact soon to establish a convenient meeting between us."

"Premier Ling," began President Miller, "we're also very grateful to have the situation resolved and await Ambassador Wen's call."

High 5's went around the Situation Room as the President called Colonel Wright.

"Colonel, let me express the nation's heartfelt appreciation for the work at the 508th Security Group and it's readiness to serve under extreme circumstances. Please plan to come to Washington in the near future and receive a promotion from General Edwards here at the White House.

Everyone in the room cheered loudly!!

16

HONG KONG

In their apartment high above Hong Kong city center on the Island of Victoria, Chin Chin and Peter receive a phone call.

"Hello, this is your friend from Washington calling on a secure line," said the President.

Chin Chin replied, "Hello, my friend. What a pleasant surprise."

Peter came over to put the cellphone on speaker mode.

As the couple huddled near the phone, the Friend asked, "We had a recent event. I couldn't tell you while you here in Washington. The Washington Post would have incited mass hysteria."

"Yes, we've had several reports from sources we trust," replied the detective.

The President asked, "What is the feedback?"

"The SSD downlink put the lead software engineer in the control center, an MIT graduate, in a catatonic state unable to type, write or speak. He was in the middle of typing an override for the rocket's flight computer. He never finished. As a result, the computer went into an endless loop never finding an executable command. Finding none, it shut down, complete with cutting the power to the clock and payload. The rocket and warhead were inert before the SSD left the Chinese airspace."

Chin Chin continued, "And while we're still gathering evidence, two things are really clear."

"Oh?"

"Yes, it's clear that the Regime is very angry about the accident, but they are even more angry about the fact that they, with their thousands of smart students who returned from the States, didn't know how we did it. And the top officials are REALLY angry because now they must start to dismantle their multi-trillion-dollar war machine."

The President asked, "Do you mean that the Premier will actually negotiate in good earnest, even in good faith?"

Our good friend, the entire leadership depends upon this new Cold War to continue. The billboards warn the people of an eminent attack from Uncle Sam."

"So, what does this mean?" asked the Friend from Washington.

"It means the Premier must meet with you without disclosing the event that brings him to the table. And he must prolong the nuclear destruction program long enough to develop other weapons that will ultimately destroy our country."

"Why?" asked the Friend.

"The Winds of Mongolia," interjected Peter.

"What the Hell does that mean?" asked the President.

"Once a generation, the locust rain down on this country from Mongolia. They destroy all of the crops. Starvation follows and regimes are toppled. China needs a LARGE second source of food. As you know the State of Iowa and selected other areas in the Mid-West have 8-feet of topsoil. China will devour every one of our pigs. Look around, my friend. They already own the premier pork producers in America."

"So, he's not in a very good bargaining position?"

"No, but he must save face."

The voice on the telephone summed up the situation, "I understand your advice to be firm on the destruction of the weapons but generous on the trade of food stuffs in order that the country produces fewer missiles, and the Premier "saves face."

"Our Friend, you read our minds." Do you have a Chinese ancestor in your DNA?"

The trio laughed.

"My friends, you're both on alert. I will be asking you to visit me in the very near future. A Hypersonica trip is really cool isn't it?"

The telecon ended with the couple doing a "High 5" and racing each other to the refrigerator to toast with a glass of champagne.

17

DES MOINES

The President sent a Hypersonica airliner to Beijing to bring the Premier and his wife to a meeting in the capitol city of the state of Iowa, Des Moines. The entourage was provided suites in the Des Lux Hotel, a 5-star hotel on Locust Street. (The President liked the idea that the street name would remind the Chinese of the Winds of Mongolia.)

The Chinese delegation was met at the airport by the Vice President and the Ambassador. A short motorcade brought the Premier and his wife to the hotel where they were met by the President and the First Lady. The hotel was only 2-blocks from the city's Farmer's Market with its world-class products.

It took one-month of planning and preparations to get a draft missile drawdown document, modelled after the Start Agreement executed decades earlier between the United States and Russia. Articles of the Agreement included:

- Build a missile destruction plant in China
- Destroy long-range series capable of hitting Hawaii
- Allow UN inspections
- Destroy 1,000 warheads in 4-years
- Bury contaminated materials in a location near the Mongolian border
- Recycle some metals into tractor parts for farm implements

The President chose Des Moines based upon a recent conversation with the couple in Hong Kong. It would clearly show off agricultural abundancies rarely seen on Earth. He was sure the Premier would like to tour the Farmer's Market.

Round table negotiations were held in the Hotel's ballroom with its rich oak panels from the 1880's.

As the negotiations proceeded, the wives were treated to a tour of Lamoni's Amish Country Store one hour south of the city. Their lunch was famous local pork sandwiches with apple pie ala mode. Then the wives were helicoptered back to Des Moines where they laid a friendship wreath in the Robert Ray Asian Gardens on the riverfront.

During a break in the negotiations, the Premier was flown via Turbopod 80-miles west to the small town of Pella, Iowa.

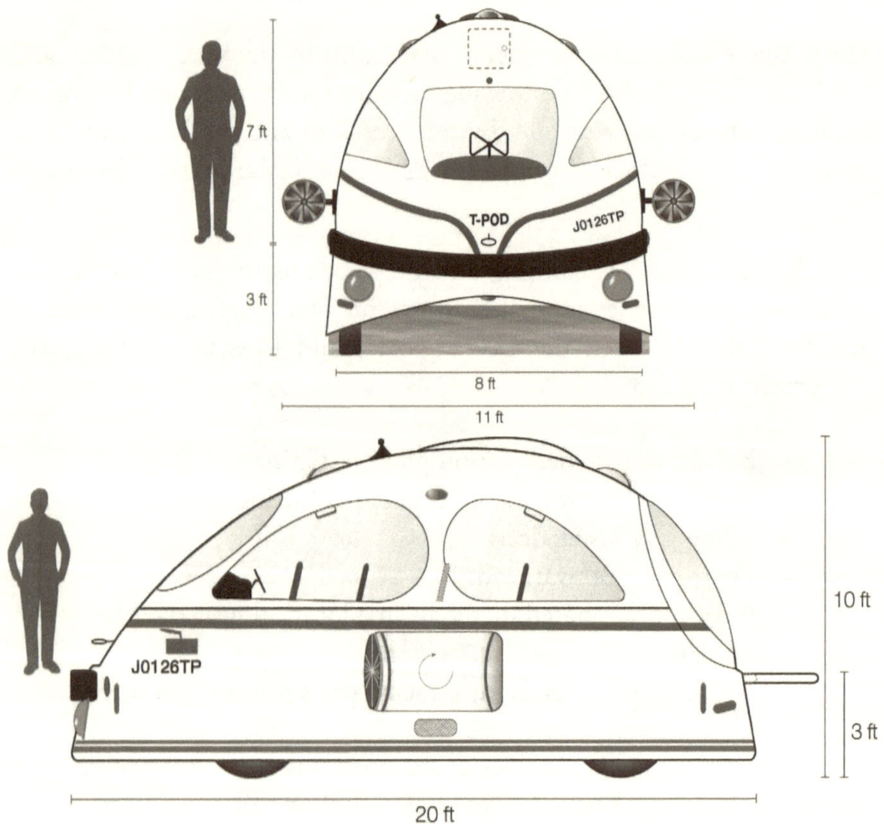

Figure 2, Turbopod

This town is a re-creation of a Dutch village with canals and fields of tulips bright in the noontime sun. The town is surrounded by seemingly endless fields of corn and soybeans. Later in the afternoon, the helicopter took the Premier to Iowa State University in Ames, considered the leading veterinary medicine school in the nation. His tour of the livestock pavilion educed many "Oh My God" reactions. His staff warned him against a show of too much enthusiasm, but the Chinese leader couldn't contain himself when he thought of the suffering the Winds of Mongolia would bring to his nation of billions of people.

For two days the negotiations continued until both parties were satisfied with the language (in both languages), and that initial objectives had been met.

President and Mrs. Miller held a state dinner for the Chinese Delegation. It was perhaps the finest 7-course dinner ever held in Amish country. The toasts seemed very sincere on both sides of the table. After the Premier and his wife excused themselves for the evening, President Miller, a native who grew up only 50 miles north and was a standout high school athlete who married his sweetheart, Barbara, hosted an after-dinner drink in the dark Oak-paneled bar with Ambassador Hinkle and his close staff.

"Well, Bruce, how are we doing?" was the President's question to his Ambassador."

Ambassador Hinkle was quick to answer, "Sir, this is perfect setting to make an impression which, fostered over the next few years, can change the course of history. In the past, a Russian President came here to Iowa or went to California and put on a cowboy hat. The impact of such meetings like this is real, and when properly managed, can last a generation."

The President took a sip of brandy and said, "Dammit, Bruce, you always say the right things!"

The insiders around the table knew the President was right.

-//-

The next morning a document signing proved to be a press bonanza for both leaders. A short Press Conference was held at the nearby airport.

As the Premier was boarding the Hypersonica aircraft with metal replica the American Flag bolted to the side (at Mach 5 any paint would disappear immediately), the Premier waved "Good Bye" and disappeared into the craft.

An hour later, as Air Force One was entering an active runway for the flight back to Washington, the President received a decoded text: "Hong Kong salutes three perfect days in Iowa."

President Miller smiled, and as he reached for his wife's hand, said, "We did good, Honey. We did very good!"

18

WHITE HOUSE II

For the second time in a month, the Detective Couple from Hong Kong checked into the Blair House and again requested the Winston Churchill suite. After she put her luggage on a rack, Chin Chin checked the schedule of events:

- 5 PM: Award Ceremony
- 6 PM: Reception
- 7 PM: Black Tie Dinner
- 9:30: Post-Dinner Reception in Library

After lunch, the couple took a 2-mile run around the Lincoln Memorial and the Washington Monument. Along the way, Chin Chin found the name of a relative on the Vietnam Wall.

They calmed down with some yoga stretches in the parlor of the suite, then rolled together into an erotic clinch which ended in a happy ending. They showered, took a quick nap and then dressed for the evening.

-//-

At 4:40 PM, a limousine picked up the couple for the obligatory one and one-half block ride to the White House.

They were greeted by the President and the First Lady and escorted to the East Ballroom. As they entered the room, a large audience rose to its feet and applauded. The President motioned for them to join the First Lady in the front row.

The President went to the podium and began to speak, "Ladies and Gentlemen, the First Lady and I are so happy you could join us on this special occasion. One of the most pleasant duties as your President is to award the Presidential Medal of Freedom to deserving citizens who have served our Republic in a most extraordinary manner. So, with your permission, I wish to read portions of this citation:

- Twenty years of the most accurate intelligence for multiple government agencies
- Key roles in classified projects
- Aide in negotiations with Asian leaders.

Our recent negotiations with Premier Ling were successful in large measure because of the insight provided by these two Americans." President Miller pointed to Chin Chin and Peter.

In turn, Chin Chin and Peter were invited to the stage where the President tied the Medal of Freedom around their necks. A brief joint speech of gratitude for the opportunity to serve followed.

Only one-half hour after entering the Ballroom, the crowd filed out to the Diplomatic Reception Room for the Reception Line. With the medals around their necks, the Chinese couple were truly gracious while glowing in the spotlight. The SecDef hugged Chin Chin and called her "an instrumental part of his inner staff."

Ambassador Hinkle posed for a picture with the couple saying: "They are like a son and daughter to me! They made my job in China so much easier!"

Right on schedule, the awardees were escorted into the State Dining Room where Chin Chin and Peter were seated at the head table in front of the podium. The President spoke about a new Sino-American Era of Friendship. He reported on missile destruction progress and subsequent trade agreements. During the entire evening the word "Dragon" was never mentioned.

After a half-hour of dancing, the couple was invited to the library for a cozy setting including the SecDef and his wife, Ambassador Hinkle and his wife, Mary, and a couple key intelligence officials with whom the couple had closely worked. California brandy was served as almost-war stories circled the room. Each version was personal and quite powerful.

It was midnight when the honored couple returned to Blair House. They were soon warm and cozy under the covers of the Churchill bed as Chin Chin thought to herself: "How lucky I am to be part of America's mission to save the world from dictators on behalf of liberty, free-trade and prosperity."

In the morning, the couple discovered a hand-written note from the President on their breakfast table. It read: "Please enjoy an all-expense Honeymoon (you never had one) in Bermuda. Your airplane is waiting at Dulles, and your suite is waiting at the Rosedon Hotel. Thank you again, and may God bless you both."

19

HONEYMOON

At noon the Gulfstream G650 ER landed at the International Airport in Bermuda. A short limo ride took the couple to downtown Hamilton where that checked into the Rosedon Hotel on Pitt's Bay Road. The doorman met the limo and welcomed the guests, "Welcome Chin Chin and Peter, we've been expecting you!"

Chin Chin looked at her partner with a "this is going to really be good" look in her eye!

The Front Desk Captain also welcomed them and said that their luggage was already on its way to the Honeymoon Suite.

"Robert, here, will show you the way and demonstrate all of the amenities in the room. He will be your personal valet while you're here. And please return here in one-half hour for a complimentary lunch."

As the new "celebrities" were finishing lunch, a tall man in a Captain's uniform entered the lobby and approached the table.

"Chin Chin and Peter, I presume," said the striking stranger.

"Yes, Sir, we are they, and with whom do we have the pleasure of speaking?" asked Chin Chin.

"My name is Win Parker. I am Harbormaster here in Hamilton. My partner, Janice Griffith, and I would like to take you on a Turbopod tour of the Islands on behalf of the management of the Micronation "Americo", the ultramodern Island Republic you saw when you landed."

Figure 3 MICRONATIONS Cover Graphic in Black & White

"Oh, yes, I remember looking out the window and wondering what that was," replied Peter.

"If you're willing, the Republic will be the last stop on our tour," said the Harbormaster.

Chin Chin and Peter looked at each other and nodded their approval.

"Fine, so please follow me to the courtyard, "said the Captain. "Oh, you don't have to pay for lunch. Remember what the President said. "All expenses paid. You are our special guests, and we're honored to have you here."

The trio walked out of the hotel into the courtyard where a bright yellow and blue Turbopod was sitting on the grass beyond the swimming pool.

As they walked up to the craft, a woman stepped out from the pilot's seat.

Win said, "Chin Chin and Peter, please meet my partner, Janice Griffith, our pilot this afternoon. Don't worry, Janice is an expert. She flew these things in the Marine Corp!"

The couples shook hands and got into the T-Pod. The side-mounted turboprop engines started, rotated to a vertical position, and within seconds, the craft rose straight up to 150-feet. It hovered for a few seconds, and then the engines rotated to their horizontal position, as Janice accelerated southwest over the city toward the Harbor. Win knew every square foot of the island chain and proved to be an excellent guide for the Honeymooners. Only the President and perhaps the former President, Matt Flynn, the inventor of the T-Pod and founder of the Americo Republic Micronation, got such a royal tour.

At 4:00 PM, Janice adroitly landed the T-Pod on the heliport of the tallest building in the new Republic. With the craft securely tied down and the Red Box anti-gravity device secure in Janice's right hand, the foursome walked into the SkyLounge. They were greeted by the Director of Sales for the Republic and given a walk-around tour of a display model of the city of the 50,000-person island democracy, one of 4 in the world created by Former President Flynn and Prince Latif of Dubai.

While having a local Pimm's Cup #4 cocktail, Win and Janice got acquainted with their new Chinese friends and shared stories on how the couples met and some of their life's adventures. It was clear that a mutual friendship could come quite easily for the two couples.

As the they were leaving the SkyLounge, Win took Chin Chin and Peter over to a floor-to-ceiling window with a southern view. He pointed out a small lagoon where he and Janice love to picnic and swim.

"We'd be honored if you would join us at the lagoon for a picnic lunch and swim tomorrow," said the dashing Harbormaster.

Chin Chin looked at Peter who nodded his approval of the idea. "OK, sounds fun," replied Chin Chin.

"Great," replied Win. "We'll pick you up at noon. That way you can be typical tourists in the morning and walk around the heart of the Hamilton only 2-blocks from the Rosedon. Wristwatches are a bargain, but everything else is expensive."

The foursome laughed as they got into the T-Pod, and Janice secured the Red Box in the console between the front seats.

Only 7-minutes later, the T-Pod landed behind the hotel. The couples shook hands and looked forward to the next day.

-//-

Late in the morning of the next day, Chin Chin and Peter packed two backpacks and went out into the court and awaited their new-found friends. Right on time, a T-Pod came over the Hotel and landed on the grass. There were a lot of T-Pods in Bermuda, but this one was the only one with special permission to land at the Rosedon. With the craft on the ground, a hotel staff member checked the serial number on the side and gave Janice the thumb's-up sign.

The couples were all smiles as the Chinese guests climbed into the back seats. Janice again showed her piloting skills as the T-Pod skimmed across the Bay and landed on the little lagoon at Americo. She steered the craft to shore where it was beached for the luncheon.

The couples donned their bathing suits and jumped off the fantail into the warm clear water. They often floated on the surface and watched small schools of fish below. The "Dirty Old Man" Harbormaster was impressed on how well the little Chinese beauty filled out her bikini. After 20-minutes, he called them to the beach where he had set up a royal lunch on a blanket under a Banyan tree. He popped the cork on a bottle of Dom Perignon champagne and served it in cut glass flutes. The four glasses clinked in a toast to world peace. The picnic basket seemed to have no bottom, but finally everyone was refusing another portion.

The next hour saw the foursome frolic in the water and sunbath on the pinkish sand. At 3:00 PM the T-Pod lifted off the water with Chin Chin at the controls and Janice beside her. She had seen them in Hong Kong and always wondered how easy it would be to fly. She was thrilled by the opportunity as Win and Peter chuckled in the backseats. She hovered over the Hotel when Janice took over and lowered the craft to the lawn. The two women did a "High 5" once the engines shut down.

The new friends parted with handshakes and hugs as Win said, "I hope you enjoy your little reception this evening."

Chin Chin asked, "Reception? I wasn't aware of any plans for this evening." She looked at Peter, "Honey, are you aware of any event?"

The Chinese gentleman merely shook his head from side to side.

As Win was getting back into the T-Pod, he smiled and said, "Don't worry my friends, you'll be in good hands." Only seconds later, the turboprops were whirling.

Back in their suite, the couple looked at their schedule only to realize that a one-hour massage was about to begin in 10-minutes.

Right on schedule, two ladies knocked on the door. They introduced themselves and quickly set up two massage tables side-by-side on the terrace of the ground floor suite. At first, Chin Chin was a bit apprehensive about the need to relax. But in only 5-minutes, her tight muscles told her to relax and enjoy the moment.

-//-

After a warm shower together, the couple took a nap with a gentle ocean breeze coming through the gauze curtains. At 5:00 PM the telephone rang. "This is your wake-up call." Chin Chin looked at Peter and asked, "Did you schedule a call, honey?"

"Not me, honey. Hell, I'm still in la-la land!"

Chin Chin reported, "Evidently, we're supposed to be in evening attire in the Lobby Bar at 5:30."

Peter was quick to say, "That works for me!"

-//-

At 5:20 the couple walked across the lobby and asked the Concierge to put their newly purchased Patek Philippe wristwatches in the safe. He obliged and alerted them that a couple friends were in the Bar waiting for them. Chin Chin, elegant in a navy-blue silk pants suit, led her partner to the Bar entrance.

"SURPRISE!! Rang out as the couple entered the Bar. Chin Chin put her hands up to her face with her mouth open in a sheer reaction. Peter immediately smiled as he recognized many of the people in front of the couple. Chin Chin and Peter made their way through the narrow passage way to the back of the establishment with its symmetrically-curved window alcove. As the shocked couple approached the end table, President Miller and the First Lady stood up. It was a total-shock reunion. They shook hands and hugged in genuine friendship. The President motioned for the Chinese couple to turn around. Of course, they followed his direction. Another cheer went up as four more people entered the Lounge. Making their way to the end of the narrow room were two elder Chinese couples…"OH MY GOD" screamed Chin Chin, "Peter, it's our parents!" The six people hugged in the middle of the room surrounded by friends with tears of joy in their eyes.

President Miller than asked for quiet as he announced the schedule, "My Friends, we will toast at our next destination. Please assemble in the lobby for our transfer to it."

-//-

In the lobby, the six excited Chinese-Americans broke into their native language. Chin Chin was quick to learn that her parents loved the Hypersonica flight from Honolulu, "although we slept for most of the two hours!"

The party was divided into three groups for the Mercedes-Benz Maybach rides to the Hamilton Dock. The three limos arrived together. As the passengers got out, there were many gasps of disbelieve as they looked up at the 310 -foot Aquaclipper at the pier.

Figure 4, New Age Ark Cover Graphic in Black and White

Another invention by Matt Flynn, this magayacht with its 8-stories and 80-foot beam, could skim across the ocean at 300 MPH, thanks to the Red Box. Normally it carries 300 passengers in sheer luxury. This night there would be only a couple dozen. The ship would overnight in Hamilton and then accept passengers for a return journey to Charleston, South Carolina, where the ship would undergo a 6-month refit. On the bow were the Skipper, Tom "Catfish" Crowley and his wife, Cathy, waving to come aboard.

-//-

And with real excitement, the party used an escalator to board the ship. They were welcomed by the First Mate and escorted to the Elevator. Every wall seemed to glisten with jewels and tiny specks of light. Peter whispered in Chin Chin's ear, "Darling, you look ravishing; I love you." She squeezed his hand in delight.

The party followed the President to the Captain's mess on the upper deck at the bow of the ship. Captain Crowley and his First Mate warmly welcomed the President and the First Lady. Then it was Chin Chin and Pete's turn, who intern introduced their parents. It wasn't too soon for tears of joy to flow. Next to be introduced were Secretary Edwards and his wife, Kim, who commented that she usually was seasick, and was glad they were in port. Ambassador Hinkle and his wife Mary were next. They had actually sailed on a Royal Caribbean cruise with Tom as the Captain! The last couple to be introduced was Dr. Tryg Ager and his wife, Asa. The President asked the tall Norwegian couple to turn around and face the other guests.

The President then stepped forward and said, "Ladies and Gentlemen, please welcome the genius behind Project Dragon." There was a polite applause.

But Chin Chin burst from Peter's grasp and rushed to hug the couple. Her small body seemed to be enveloped by the tall couple as they hugged. The truth about the emotional moment and Ager's contribution to world peace was THE topic at dinner.

Captain Crowley stepped forward and invited the guests to join him in a Champagne toast to the Honeymooners. Stewards with silver trays passed among the guests to pass out flutes of the bubbly.

"But, wait, said the Captain to the Lead Steward in a voice everyone could hear, "Sir, there are still four glasses of Champagne. Who did you miss?"

Just then, two couples came side-by-side down the corridor to the Captain's Mess.

In the next couple of seconds, there was a communal "OH MY GOD" moment of the party. Walking directly toward the Captain were Former President Flynn and First Lady Heather and Former Madam President DeYoung and her husband, Jon.

President Miller looked at the Captain as to say, "You SOB, why didn't you tell me?"

Catfish smiled and simply said, "President Flynn swore me to secrecy!"

In the background, the secret service people dressed as waiters had a hard time watching the friendship hugging frenzy taking place in the rotunda entrance to the Mess.

The group calmed enough to toast "America and World Peace, fostered by the group assembled!"

President Miller nodded to his friend, Matt Flynn, and said, "Mr. President, this is your ship, you must have something to say."

Matt smiled at his friend and said, "We'll, Sir, all of have to say is that Heather and I are full of pride for the Honeymooners who served my administration and that of President DeYoung's, in such an outstanding manner. Thank you, Mr. President for the award to them. I hope everyone here understands the extent of this couple's contribution to our Republic. It can be summed up in a couple of words: "Earth's Survival." Please reflect on the achievement and relish this time together."

The guests were stunned to a reflective silence only to be broken by a dinner chime.

Captain Crowley led the group into the formal dining room with assigned seating at round tables. The Honeymooners sat with the Presidents and their wives/husband. The Captain entertained with sea stories at the second table with his wife and the Parents who were seasoned world travelers. The third table had the Secretary of Defense Edwards and his wife, Kim, Ambassador Hinkle and his wife, Mary, and Win and Janice and Tryg and Asa, where several found out they had relatives and hobbies in common.

The event was catered by the Rosedon. Needless to say, everyone enjoyed the cuisine and the fact that such an event was even possible with the Chinese military build-up.

-//-

During desert, President Miller, stood up to speak. "I know whatever I say could be better said by my two friends at this table. However, please allow me to try."

A polite giggle followed the remark.

The President continued, "Chin Chin and Peter, we had a lovely ceremony in the White House earlier this week. Your many friends, old and new, were sincerely grateful for your service to this proud Republic we call America. But, and this is scary true, they did not realize that just like the Apollo Mission to the moon which only had 26-seconds to find a landing place or forever be abandoned, that during the recent missile event, we only had 26-seconds to stop a nuclear chain reaction that would have eventually blotted out the Sun, the very one that's setting out that window.

So, Chin Chin and Peter, when you return to that island jewel called Hong Kong and you drive up Garden Road to the split at Conduit Road, look to your right. You will see a life-size sculpture with the both of you standing and peering though a telephoto lens north toward Kowloon and the Mainland of China which you have so diligently observed for your nation."

Genuine applause and "Bravo's" erupted.

At this point, President Miller asked Dr. Ager to stand and speak. The stately IBM executive was handed the microphone. The silence was deafening as he turned around and in a very deep measured tone said, "Ladies and Gentlemen, Project Dragon had to work during those 26-seconds. We had a back-up, but it may have been too late. So, we are very lucky to be here celebrating this couple and the many achievements of the members of this august body (the Doctor swung his arm around to indicate the entire audience), but, and here's my take-away for this evening. It reminds us of the role that luck, just like what the astronauts needed or what we needed to find the perfect mate, the role that luck plays in everybody's life and, indeed, in the life of the planet."

There wasn't a dry eye in the room for many good reasons!